Alfred Gurney

Voices from the Holy Sepulchre

And other Poems

Alfred Gurney

Voices from the Holy Sepulchre
And other Poems

ISBN/EAN: 9783337206536

Printed in Europe, USA, Canada, Australia, Japan

Cover: Foto ©Andreas Hilbeck / pixelio.de

More available books at **www.hansebooks.com**

VOICES

FROM THE

HOLY SEPULCHRE

AND OTHER POEMS

.

BY

ALFRED GURNEY, M.A.

VICAR OF S. BARNABAS', PIMLICO

AUTHOR OF 'A CHRISTMAS FAGGOT' ETC.

LONDON

KEGAN PAUL, TRENCH, & CO., 1 PATERNOSTER SQUARE

1889

TO THE DEAR MEMORY

OF

EDMUND GURNEY

WITH A BROTHER'S LOVE

PREFACE

THE WELCOME given to 'A Christmas Faggot' encourages me to publish a few more poems. The present is a sister-volume to that, and my wish has been that its dominant note might be an echo, true however faint, of the Easter 'Alleluia!'

My thanks are again due to my friend Mr. SHIELDS for the frontispiece—another of his lovely picture-poems.

CONTENTS

a

ALLELUIA! ALLELUIA! ALLELUIA!

'Opens a Door in Heaven;
　From skies of glass
　A Jacob's ladder falls
　On greening grass,
　And o'er the mountain-walls
　　Young Angels pass.'—*Tennyson.*

'Waft of soul's wing!
　What lies above?
　Sunshine and Love,
　　Skyblue and Spring!'—*Browning.*

'Lost, lost are all our losses;
　Love set for ever free;
The full life heaves and tosses
　Like an eternal sea!
One endless living story!
　One poem spread abroad!
And the sun of all our glory
　Is the countenance of GOD.'—*Novalis.*

'Rise, heart; thy Lord is risen.　Sing his praise
　Without delays,
Who takes thee by the hand that thou likewise
　With him mayst rise.'
　　　　　　　　　　　George Herbert.

'My Beloved spake and said unto me, Rise up, my love, my fair one, and come away.　For, lo, the Winter is past, the rain is over and gone; the flowers appear on the earth; the time of the singing of birds is come, and the voice of the turtle is heard in our land.　The fig tree putteth forth her green figs and the vines with the tender grape give a good smell.　Arise, my love, my fair one, and come away.'—*Solomon's Song.*

I.

THE GOSPEL OF THE RESURRECTION.

THE Sleeper from His bed,

Uplifts His Royal Head,

His Footfall is sweet music to the ear

Of angels who discern

The signs of His Return,

While Rome's all-conquering soldiers quake with

fear.

B

Like dead men they become

Those veterans of Rome,

Trembles the world to which such tools belong ;

All powerless their strength,

A Righteous King at length

Uplifts the Sceptre that alone is strong.

The women-mourners weep,

They know not death is sleep,

A sleep ordained the sleeper to renew ;

Yet, spite of their despair,

Sweet ointments they prepare,

One service still remains for them to do.

Sad, through the garden-gloom,

They hasten to the Tomb,

The grave wherein their hopes all buried lie ;

And find with glad dismay

The great stone rolled away ;

Death and despair—these are the things that die.

And is He then alive ?

And may their hopes revive ?

His Easter greeting falls upon their ear ;

Ah yes ! they know that voice,

Well may their hearts rejoice,

By love possest, the love that conquers fear.

All fears be put to flight !

'T is death that dies outright—

Nor may the darkness with the light compete ;

The stone on every tomb

Is ready to become

A preacher's pulpit, and an angel's seat.

Now earth with all its blooms

Its music, its perfumes,

God's cloister is, encompassing the shrine

Where men and angels meet

The Risen Lord to greet,

Whose Presence turns earth's water into wine.

They camp on holy ground,

They pitch their tents around

The sheltering Pavilion of their King ;

The love-feast is begun

Of God and man at one ;

The Morning Stars uplift their voice and sing.

Nuremberg : 1889.

II.

A MESSAGE.

WHEREVER Christians lay their dead
   Christ's Sepulchre they build ;
Death is for them interpreted,
   And hope not unfulfilled.

The highest, brightest hopes alone
   Have reason on their side ;
'T is death itself that dies, o'erthrown
   By Jesus Crucified.

He tasted it ; its impotence

    To harm Him was made plain ;

So ended was the long suspense,

    The fear of death was slain.

Beyond the tomb mine eyes have gazed,

    And from the other side

I heard a voice (may God be praised !)

    A voice that testified :—

‘ The Conqueror, His Promise kept,

    Has put an end to strife ;

The one you loved, the one you wept,

    Has faded into life.

‘ The face has vanished ; not the grace

 That made the face a shrine,

Where loyal love was wont to trace

 A signature divine.

‘ The presence seems a thing withdrawn ;

 In truth it is not so ;

More tender than the opening dawn

 Is evening’s afterglow.

 ‘ If flowers fade, by heart and hand

 The gift shall be renewed ;

Ah, then shall lovers understand

 Love’s full beatitude !

' Each loss shall be at last retrieved,

And each reverse reversed,

And blithe shall be each heart bereaved

More blithe than at the first—

' When marriage-bells again ring out

A bridal morn to greet ;

And Angels and Archangels shout,

As parted lovers meet.'

We turn to gain all seeming loss

If but His Rod be kissed,

Who in the shadow of the Cross

Ordained the Eucharist.

Whenever Christians mourn their dead

They stand Christ's Tomb beside,

There see they death interpreted,

Transfigured, glorified !

III.

AN APPEAL.

HARK to the Bride's—the Spirit's—call !

Accomplished is Love's enterprise ;

Man's doom is not to rise and fall,

He dies to live, he falls to rise.

Let love to faith her succour bring ;

With beating heart and kindling eye,

Let hope lift up her voice and sing

The song that is a prophecy.

O gather, ye who know Him not,

 The Sepulchre of Christ around,

Where Firstfruits in a small seed-plot

 The patient Husbandman has found.

Come, see the place where Jesus lay

 For evermore untenanted ;

Its emptiness proclaims alway

 That death henceforth is captive led.

Behold the Tomb whence Jesus rose,

 Triumphant o'er the Gates of Hell ;

Still mighty to subdue His foes,

 Through patient love invincible.

Mark how from age to age His Bride

Uplifts that yearning heart of hers,

And, dauntless, keeps her watch beside

Earth's still unopened sepulchres.

Upon her prayers His Blessing waits

Till all their captives are set free ;

Her soaring hope anticipates

His death-destroying Victory.

A Shepherd He who wearies not

Of seeking till the lost are found ;

A Sower of each barren spot,

Till the whole earth be harvest-ground.

NEUHAUSEN : 1889.

IV.

A CAROL.

BRIGHTLY burn the tapers tall,
  High the fragrant censer swings,
Hasten to the Banquet-hall,
  Hark ! what news the Angel brings !
Jesus, rising, raises all
  On His Easter-wings.

Open is the Tomb to-day,
  Empty is the charnel-bed ;

See the place where Jesus lay,

 He is risen as He said ;

Well He knows the homeward way,

 ' Free among the dead.'

Birds their happy music make,

 Flowers blossom at His feet ;

All creation seems to wake

 With a laughter soft and sweet ;

Ne'er did morn so blithely break

 Weeping eyes to greet.

Ah ! it is no idle tale

 Women to Apostles tell ;

They have heard the sweet ' All hail '

In a voice remembered well.

Mighty is He to prevail

Over death and hell.

Mighty is He to console,

Mighty to emancipate,

Strong to make the sick heart whole,

Strong to cleanse and consecrate,

Whose Uprising makes life's goal

Heaven's open gate.

Now may all His children say

' Death is disinherited ' ;

Christ, the new and living Way,

    Christ, the true and living Bread,

Proudly we proclaim to-day

    ' Firstborn from the Dead ! '

Brightly burn the tapers tall,

    High the fragrant censer swings,

Angels crowd the Banquet-hall,

    Holy Church in triumph sings ;

'T is the crowning Festival

    Of the King of Kings.

S. BARNABAS' : *Easter Day*, 1888.

HOMEWARD BOUND.

Up the Mount of Aspiration,
  For our native highlands bound,
Climb we ; only at the summit
  May a resting-place be found,
Where, above this shifting cloudland,
  Love is throned and crowned.

For that summit is the Centre,
  And that throne the Mercy-seat ;

All who in His Footsteps follow,

Broken hearts and bleeding feet,

There at length shall rest securely,

There at length shall meet.

Blessed are the swift forerunners,

Leaders of our pilgrim band ;

Faint, but in their steps pursuing,

We with them at length shall stand,

Recreated, reunited,

In our Fatherland.

Ascension Day, 1885.

LIFE'S TRANSFIGURATION.

' How merrily the throstle sings,

    The sun is bright, the world is gay ;—

    For me the year has lost its May,

And joy and hope are banished things.'

'T was thus I sang long years ago ;

    My life a wreck, my song a sigh ;

    I did not know the wish to die

Is born of death, as now I know.

For love, sore threatened, still survives ;

 A swimmer on a stormy sea,

 Intrepid, resolute, is he,

More vigorous the more he strives.

Kind sorrow's consecrating hands

 Were laid upon my head ; 't was well ;

 Life issues from a broken shell,

The stricken heart alone expands.

Life issues from a buried seed ;

 The sigh is prelude to the song ;

 The lover needs, to make him strong,

The discipline by love decreed.

The chastisement that death ordains

Must be by love interpreted ;

Who bends the knee and bows the head

On high is lifted up and reigns.

Love's feast a vigil must precede ;

The coming rapture who can tell,

The offspring of the broken shell,

The outcome of the buried seed ?

The silent throstle folds her wings,

The sun has set, the world grows grey ;

But all the year for me is May,

My heart for very gladness sings.

BAYREUTH : *Feast of the Transfiguration*, 1889.

GLIMPSES.

SOMETIMES my prisoned spirit throws

Its fetters off, my heart expands,

The golden gate half open stands,

The woven veil transparent grows.

The music wafted from above

Falls softly on half-opened ears,

And, ere the Vision disappears,

I almost see the Face I love.

Enough! in patience let me wait,

Expecting till it come again;

Then may the veil be rent in twain!

Then may I pass the open gate!

SWITZERLAND: 1889.

UNDERTONES.

(To E. M. G.)

'T IS a loud world, a noisy throng :

    Loud are the voices of the crowd,

    Loud are the market-cries, and loud

The soldiers' march, the feasters' song.

But other sounds there are that bring

    A softer music to the ear

    Opened by sympathy to hear

The world's pathetic whispering.

I pray you, mark the undertones:

    Soft is the mother's lullaby,

    Gentle the love-lorn maiden's sigh,

And faint the sick man's dying moans.

A low and humble voice is theirs

    Who in the place of penance kneel,

    And all their shame and grief reveal

With tears more eloquent than prayers.

How wondrously a still small voice,

    Charged with a consecrating word,

    Makes its sublime announcement heard,

While silent worshippers rejoice.

The nuptial vows of man and maid

    Are softly spoken, as they stand

    Before God's Altar, and her hand

All silently in his is laid.

The kiss that only two can hear—

    Is any sound more soft than this?

    Yes, softer than the lovers' kiss,

Is the lone widow's falling tear.

And softer sounds perchance than these

    Visit the ears of dying men,

    The Angels' welcome,—soft as when

Sweet zephyrs kiss the Summer seas.

The undertones of Nature keep

    Their magic secret ; sun and star

    And wind and wave, all vocal are,

Each flower sings itself to sleep.

Each month brings whispers of its own ;

    Soft is the rain-cloud's overflow,

    And soft a footfall on the snow,

Each season has its undertone.

To those who fondly study her

    Nature is ever musical,

    Her sweetest notes the softest fall,

The sea-shell is a whisperer.

Her music, day by day renewed,

    Is oftentimes an undersong,

    And echoes faint the spell prolong.

With silence for an interlude.

The world is full of loud debate

    In senate, market-place and street,

    Deaf to the whispers sad and sweet,

The voices inarticulate.

Oh, for a sympathetic ear,

    Companion to a heart that feels !

    A mystery itself reveals

In all we see, in all we hear.

And, if there be one voice alone

　　Whose music thrills you through and through,

　　The charm that so entrances you,

Say, is it not an undertone ?

SCHAFFHAUSEN : 1889.

FOOTPRINTS ON THE ATLANTIC.

FOOTPRINTS on the broad Atlantic

    Let us reverently trace ;

Pilgrim-footsteps moving westward,

    Men of every creed and race,

Seeking, till the restless waters

    Yield a resting place.

Westward moves the great procession,

    Westward still, whate'er befall ;

So the father of the faithful

Shaped his course, for God did call ;

Westward rode the Magi, westward

Swelled the sails of Paul.

Through long years men questioned, wondered,

(Hope must doubt and fear outrun),

Hide the western waves a treasure

Buried 'neath the setting sun ?

Came at length the great Adventure,

And the prize was won !

By a phantom fleet encompassed,

Steer we for the fabled West ;

From the foremost prow Columbus,

Hope-enkindled, faith-possest,

Points us forward, self-devoted

To a sacred quest.[1]

Steal across the sea at sundown

Fragments of a sacred song ;

'T is the vesper hymn to Mary,

Heard the winds and waves among,

Sung by Spanish sailors ; sea-nymphs

Still the strain prolong.

England's heroes quickly follow,

And the English flag is seen

[1] *See* Note A.

Traversing the stormy waters

   Which 'twixt two worlds intervene,

Claiming the discovered country

   For her virgin-queen.

In their wake another vessel

   Sails, a blossom on the wave ;[1]

Exiles are the hearts that man her,

   Pilgrim-fathers, stern and brave,

Making for a land of freedom,

   Or a salt sea grave.

Voices raised in loud defiance,

   On Atlantic breezes borne,

[1] The ' Mayflower.'

Tell of strife ; the quarrel ended,

    Breaks at length a brighter morn ;

Child and mother face each other,

    Love subduing scorn.

Footprints on the broad Atlantic,

    Be it yours and mine to trace ;

Westward still the great procession

    Travels ;—one in creed and race,

May America and England

    Evermore embrace !

ON BOARD THE 'AURANIA': *August*, 1885.

SPAIN'S CRUSADE.[1]

'Castilian gentlemen
Choose not their task, they choose to do it well.'
GEORGE ELIOT, *Spanish Gypsy.*

THOUGH many thousand miles away,

In this old city, once again

Is wafted to my ears to-day

A whisper from the shores of Spain.

The stars and stripes have disappeared ;

A prouder banner is unfurled,

The standard once renowned and feared

On battle-fields of the old world.

[1] *See* Note B.

Another Santa Fé I see,

    And—fairest pageant ever seen—

Spain's noblest, proudest chivalry

    Marshalled around their King and Queen.

Up to Granada's walls they ride,

    Met by the vanquished Moorish King ;

Behind Abdallah open wide

    The gates to Christians entering.

Breaks his sad heart with one last sigh ;

    Ne'er shall the Crescent rise again ;

The Alhambra Towers lift on high

    The Cross of Christ, the flag of Spain.

Te Deum is the triumph-song

    Sung by the prostrate victor-host,

A burst of music loud and long,

    To Father, Son, and Holy Ghost.

Thus, to her high commission true,

    Did Spain her destiny fulfil ;

Her knights were born this work to do,

    Her ladies are crusaders still.

Santa Fé, New Mexico : 1885.

THE MOUNTAIN OF THE HOUSE OF THE LORD.

' In the last days it shall come to pass that the mountain of the House of the Lord shall be established in the top of the mountains, and it shall be exalted above the hills ; and people shall flow unto it.'

GOD'S House a lofty mountain is,

A holy, happy Home, wherein

His sons and daughters taste the bliss

Of life that knows no sin.

Established is this citadel,

The sanctuary of truth and grace ;

Gathered therein Love's vassals dwell,

Oh, 't is a wealthy place !

God's handiwork ! exalted high,

   Of Love's own loveliness fulfilled ;

Mighty is He to beautify

   What He alone can build.

God's mountain-top ! the nations flow

   Through gates that ever open stand ;

Upward is ever homeward ; so

   Gain we our Fatherland.

Here in this beauty-haunted spot,

   Discerning ' shadows of the True,'

I pluck this one forget-me-not,

   And give it, friend, to you.

Manitou, Colorado: 1885.

THE NEW WORLD.

'That new world which is the old.'
                              TENNYSON.

A NEW world did Columbus find?

Ah! 't is not so *that* world is found;

God's golden harvest-sheaves who bind

Are tillers of another ground.

No new world like the old we need;

One thing suffices—one alone,

A garnered world-harvest from seed

The wounded Hands of Christ have sown.

No earthly Paradise avails,

    No Eldorado in the West ;

The Spirit's Breath must fill their sails

    Who seek the Highlands of the Blest.

By stripes is healing wrought, and stars

    Point ever to a central Sun ;

He flies the conquering flag, whose scars,

    Transfigured, speak of Victory won.

O Royal Heart, Thy Kingdom come !

    All else may change ; all else may go :

Not eastward, westward, is our Home,

    But *onward, upward* :—even so !

One Sign alone is love-designed,

God's Evergreen, the·Eternal Rood ;

Happy the home-seekers who find

Its meaning plain—*a world renewed*!

OFF THE COAST OF IRELAND : *November*, 1885.

RALPH WALDO EMERSON.

' Happiness in labour, righteousness, and veracity ; in all the
life of the spirit ; happiness and eternal hope ;—that was Emerson's
gospel.'—MATTHEW ARNOLD.

NOT with the seers his niche, nor where

Wisdom enshrined uplifts her torch ;

But in the balmy, sunlit air

Of Truth's wide open temple-porch.

Hers was his harp ; his heart was hers ;

And hence his mission cannot fail,

Interpreting the characters

Inwoven on the outer veil.

'T was hidden manna that he sought,

His pilgrimage was one ascent ;

With mystery and meaning fraught

To him was Nature's sacrament.

May men to larger stature grow,

May greener laurels still be won ;

Yet flowers ever fresh shall blow

Upon the grave of Emerson.

CALIFORNIA : 1885.

HENRI FRÉDÉRIC AMIEL.

'Notre ami était de ceux qu'a touchés de son aile l'ange des visions ineffables et des divines tristesses.'—EDMOND SCHERER.

O BROTHER-SOUL! how well thy moods I know,

Thy yearnings strong, thy scruples manifold,

By doubt made timid, and by love made bold ;

With pain I mark thy deep heart's overflow,

Pain born of sympathy ; I seem to go

Along thy shadowed path, thy hand to hold,

With fears and hopes commingled, uncontrolled,

A baffled wanderer in a world of snow.

But white that world, and with horizons vast ;

And white thy soul with wistful eyes that scan

The heights, the depths, the Future and the Past,

The Names of God, the destinies of man ;

Sweet tearful eyes ! they shall be blithe at last,

When Love concludes and crowns what Love

began.

BAYREUTH : 1889.

JOHN HENRY NEWMAN.

'Forgive me that I love you as I do.'
AUBREY DE VERE.

HAVE I not loved thee? felt the magic spell

Of eloquence so sober and so sweet,

Of thought so subtle, knowledge so complete,

Profound, intuitive, of things that dwell

Far-hidden in the soul's most secret cell,

Where thought and feeling at their sources meet,

And Conscience sits upon her royal seat,

Whose golden sceptre is a sword as well?

'Father' I fain would call thee, but a chill,

   Heartfelt, arrests me if I call thee so ;

   That sacred name my lips must still forego,

Yet all the more my heart shall love thee still.

With thee I bend the knees of heart and will ;

   How I have loved thee, thou wilt one day know.

SWITZERLAND : 1889.

SALUTATIONS.

I.

IN THE NAME OF THE GOD OF PEACE.

(TO EDWARD, LORD BISHOP OF LINCOLN.)

PEACE ! is it not the Master's own bequest ?

   The peace-makers are blessed evermore ;

   Their home they have within the heavenly door.

But here their work, where all is still unrest.

This be thy lovely task—at love's behest,

   The Pentecostal music to restore ;

   Babel is doomed, but it must fall before

Jerusalem in peace can be possest.

Thy pastoral heart,—so burdened with the care

    Of struggling souls thou fain wouldst fold and

    feed,

With Apostolic toil and strenuous prayer

So exercised,—this special cross must bear,

    To suffer for the Church's ancient Creed ;

    Peace-loving hearts are still the hearts that

    bleed.

BAYREUTH : *Feast of the Holy Name*, 1889.

II.

IN THE NAME OF THE GOD OF HOPE.

A TRUCE to sickly doubt, and fear's suspense!

   Now bring we gold and frankincense and myrrh

   To Him, of love, of life, the Cherisher,

With homage of undoubting confidence.

Be love its own sufficient recompense;

   The darkest night is day's mute harbinger;

   The trusting soul, when sorrow visits her,

Has God —yea, God Himself—for her defence.

My heart more weary is than weary feet,

And closed and distant seems the heavenly

door,

Foundations tremble that seemed firm before.—

A truce to doubt !—Beloved, 't will be sweet,

With hearts made true and tender to the core,

Upon the ramparts of God's House to meet.

July, 1889.

CATHOLIC ASSURANCE.

COURAGE! my soul, possess thyself in peace ;

   Though love grows cold, and few there be who

      wait

   With eyes uplifted to the heavenly gate,

Expecting till Christ's advent brings release ;

Though love-denying heresies increase,

   Surrender not thy hope, anticipate

   His sure Return, whose word shall recreate

A world grown old, and bid contention cease.

Thine ear, so sorely wounded with the strife

   Of clamorous tongues, one touch of His can

      heal,

   Whose hasty servant at the Paschal meal,

The feast of love, had armed him with a knife,

   And struck at Malchus with misguided zeal ;

Rebuked by Him who gives—who is—the Life.

NUREMBERG : 1889.

DUALITY.

'I sleep, but my heart waketh.'

MY soul's companion has a keener sense,

    More truly marks, more clearly registers,

    The thing I see, the thought that in me stirs ;

She will inform me when I journey hence,

What means my life's turmoil,—experience

    Strangely the same, yet not the same, as hers.

    For still my slumbering consciousness defers

Its answer to the questions ' why ' and ' whence.'

Indweller! though so distant seems the goal,

Not uncompanioned shall my pilgrim-soul

    Its *via dolorosa* still pursue ;

Self-questioning, when I my life review,

From fragments seeking to forecast the whole,

    I find myself in colloquy with you.[1]

NUREMBERG : 1889.

[1] *See* Note C.

TO LILIAN.

'Every beloved object is the centre of a paradise.'—NOVALIS.

LOVE puts a sceptre in your hand,

Upon your head a crown ; you stand

The queen of an enchanted land.

Methinks your soldier-lover, who

Ne'er trembled when his sword he drew,

Will tremble when he kisses you.

So proud upon his breast to wear,

Among the stars that sparkle there,

A lily, finding it more fair.

The sword his hand has learnt to wield

On many a well-fought battle-field

Your lips will kiss—(so Lancelot's shield

Was fondled by ' the lily-maid,'

A sister-lily !)—not afraid

Of blood-stains on a soldier's blade.

Two worlds you shall together win,

Glory without and grace within ;

A hero weds a heroine.

A soldier's life is dedicate ;

Strong angel-guardians with you wait

To crown him at a golden gate—

The gate of Honour,—brave and true

And tender all who ride therethrough ;

Such may your lover be to you !

Then in the happy years to come,

Where'er your feet may chance to roam,

Your heart in his shall find a home.

Thus heart in heart and hand in hand,

Love shall increase, and life expand ;

Before you lies the Promised Land !

Michaelmas, 1888.

TO STELLA.

'Innocence hath privilege in her
To dignify arch looks, and laughing eyes.'

WORDSWORTH.

'T IS a vision I have seen—

Spring with magic powers

Turns a wintry landscape green,

Makes a world of flowers.

Laughs a golden crocus there,

Summer's glow forestalling ;

Smiles a snowdrop pale and fair,

Winter's gleam recalling.

Happy nurslings of the Spring

Dance in leafy bowers ;

Sing the song the fairies sing—

' Wonderland is ours.'

In the sky the flowers are

Fairer still and sweeter ;

Shines for me a rosy star,

And I come to greet her.

Smiles for me a dimpled face

Bashfully audacious,

Centre of a world of grace,—

Stella the all-gracious !

Easter, 1889.

SUNDRY KINDS OF DEATH.

FOUR PAGES OF AN OLD ALBUM.

FIRST PAGE.

Laura.

YOU see a lady there whose hand

So lightly touched the sweet guitar,

So daintily ; I oft would stand,—

Her casement and the evening star

Above me, while those trembling notes

Made soft response to words of mine ;

Ah, still across my memory floats

That face ! 'T were folly to repine.

But still, when toasts go gaily round,

  I pledge her reverently, and try,

Aroused by the familiar sound,

  To stifle the half-uttered sigh.

Ah ! there be sundry kinds of death,

  Each with its own significance ;

But in the end it quickeneth

  To life—to sweeter life perchance.

SECOND PAGE

Lionel.

SEE here a college friend of mine,

His the best joke, the blithest song ;

I told him once across the wine

The thing that he had done was wrong.

I could not let the matter pass,

I spoke my mind, I saw him wince,

He answered roughly, and alas !

No words have passed between us since.

I often meet him in the street,

    His eyes meet mine, those handsome eyes,

That used to flash their welcome, meet

    My own, and will not recognise.

Ah! there be sundry kinds of death,

    The vital flame burns up and sinks;

But in the end it quickeneth

    To life—to truer life methinks.

Lancelot.

BUT sweeter eyes this page adorn,

Another friend of long ago ;

I love him with a love forlorn,

He little knows I love him so.

A bosom friend ! his counsel wise

Was like a staff to lean upon ;

Till, friendly rivals, for one prize

We both competed, and I won.

He vanished ; on my marriage-day

A foreign letter made me start ;

It told me he had gone away

For ever, with a broken heart.

Ah ! there be sundry kinds of death,

It falls upon the hopes of youth ;

But in the end it quickeneth

To life—to fuller life in sooth.

FOURTH PAGE.

Leonore.

THERE smiles my queen, the loveliest,

   Her cheeks aflame with two bright spots

That tell her story ; at her breast

   Nestle some white forget-me-nots.

I keep the little glove, but oh !

   The hand that wore it never more

Shall link with mine,—alone I go

   The way that she has gone before :

Alone save by that memory cheered,

And with this hope to brace my will

That one on earth beloved, revered,

In heaven may be my darling still.

Ah ! there be sundry kinds of death,

Ashes to ashes, dust to dust ;

But in the end it quickeneth

To life—to deathless life I trust.

IN MEMORY OF JUNE, 1887.

I.

ENGLISH hearts on land and sea

Keep the queen-heart's jubilee.

England's standard floats unfurled,

Shadowing a sunlit world.

Dancing waves and winds at play

Share a nation's holiday.

Stars and birds and flowers all

Bid us keep the festival.

Children's laughter makes reply

(Laughter is a prophecy) ;

Expectation fills their eyes,

Recollecting Paradise.

Blessedly convinced are they,

Life 's a life-long holiday.

Lovers too uplift their voice,

Calling all men to rejoice.

Blithely they their witness give—

'T is a blissful thing to live.

II.

Every saint and every sage

Tell us life 's a pilgrimage.

Narrow is the path and steep,

Climbers sometimes faint and weep.

Weary oft their feet and bleeding—

Whither is the pathway leading?

Silencing all fear and doubt,

Angels answer with a shout :

' Love is king by right divine,

Turning water into wine.

' Royal-hearted if we be,

Life 's a life-long jubilee.'

Saints take up the triumph-song,

And the jubilance prolong :

' Certain is the goal,' they sing,

' In the palace of a King.'

This the moral of my rhyme—

'T is a blessed thing to climb.

III.

Evermore from age to age

Life 's a life-long pilgrimage.

So, so only, can it be

Festival and jubilee.

' Yes,' a still small voice replies,

' And e'en more,—a *sacrifice.*

' If the heart to Christ be given,

Earth 's the vestibule of heaven.

What a pageant shall we see

Keeping God's own Jubilee !

BARROW COURT.

SACRED the valley and the hill,
   The well-known meadows, gardens, trees ;
All holy ground to me, and still
   Haunted by memories.

And now a new home fronts the old,
   The smiling valley lies between,
With here and there a patch of gold,
   And lawns and pastures green.

'T is still a consecrated spot,

    Long ages past to praise and prayer

Devoted ; a forget-me-not

    Each flower blooming there.

.

Nestles in hallowed ground hard by

    A little Church, a lowly shrine,

And Churchyard Cross, where Piety

    Reveres the sacred Sign.

The many-gabled house o'erlooks

    A terraced garden, and behind

A hollow green with shady nooks

    And orchard you will find.

Beyond, a woodland path you tread,

Ascending to the lovely combe ;—

But turn we to the house instead,

And pass from room to room.

A cultured taste has set its seal

On every chamber ; all the place,

The more you know it, makes you feel

The charm of old-world grace.

Stately the hall whose deep recess

An ancient Crucifix enshrines ;

Outside and in, to cheer and bless,

Are Faith's familiar signs.

And here from many a pictured book

Sweet faces gaze, sweet voices call,—

The chamber of the ingle-nook

Within the garden-hall.

Throughout the house a welcome seems

To greet you wheresoe'er you go :

Smiles brighter than the golden beams

Of sunshine on the snow.

For one presides whose maiden-bloom

Has ripened to maternal grace ;

Her presence brightens every room,

The sunshine of the place.

Ah ! Cupid's roguish eyes were wet

With happy tears of glad import,

When Sussex gave to Somerset

The queen of Barrow Court.

And baby-laughters echo sweet

Through nursery, drawing-room, and hall ;

Beneath the dance of baby-feet

The boards ring musical.

What keeps the world for ever young,

Still mindful of its heavenly birth

Its many sepulchres among,—

What but the children's mirth ?

G

This is their high vocation, pledged

> To dissipate life's gathered glooms ;

They, they alone, are privileged

> To dance among the tombs.[1]

Their voices evermore prolong

> The music of a prophecy ;

Who knows the meaning of that song

> May sweeten grief thereby.

Unchanged the valley and the hill,

> Though much be changed.   It matters not ;

For Love is lord and master still,

> And consecrates the spot.

BARROW COURT : *May*, 1886.

[1] *See* Note D.

ROMSEY ABBEY.

My soul in many homes has dwelt,

In sunshine and in shade,

In many sanctuaries knelt,

At many altars prayed.

In many lands my heart has been,

Companioned and alone,

And here a Pisgah-sight has seen,

There found a Bethel-stone.

But to one sacred spot to-day
  My memory returns,
An English Abbey old and grey
  Towards which my spirit yearns.

A sculptured Crucifix relieves
  The southern wall ; above
An outstretched Hand bestows, receives,
  The Sacrifice of Love.

Without, within, 't is nobly planned—
  The nave so broad and high,
With pillared aisles on either hand,
  Strength crowned by majesty.

One in a low side-altar ends,

    Where oft in bygone days

A little company of friends

    Would meet for prayer and praise :

Would meet the Lord of Life to seek,

    In Him to meet *indeed* ; [1]

Like Him, with Him, for all the weak

    And sad to intercede.

'T is theirs who taste the Living Bread

    The dying to befriend ;

He whom a Father's Hands have fed

    A brother's wounds must tend.

[1] *See* Note E.

And thus the world-redeeming Name,

 Through service understood,

Lit up with Pentecostal flame,

 Declares God's Fatherhood.

Recall, my soul, those happy hours,

 And render thanks anew,

When all earth's blooms were altar-flowers,

 Bathed in baptismal dew.

Ah! Beauty never really dies,

 Because God changes not ;

Nor shall the fruitful memories

 That gather round that spot—

That sacred spot, that lowly shrine,

    Where oft in bygone years

A Hand, dispensing Bread and Wine,

    Has wiped away my tears.

My heart in many homes has dwelt,

    At many altars prayed,

But nowhere more at home has felt

    Than in that Abbey's shade.

The arduous ascent of prayer

    Leads ever to the light

That shines adown the Bethel-stair,

    And crowns the Pisgah-height.

NEUHAUSEN : *August*, 1889.

THE CHAPEL OF THE HOLY SEPULCHRE.[1]

S. BARNABAS', PIMLICO.

WHO seeks his spirit's lamp to trim

Need to no wilderness repair ;

Yet would I fain commend to him

A chosen place of prayer.

' Thy closet enter, shut the door '

Is Christ's own rubric, oft forgot ;

Where'er, whate'er, that chamber floor,

How sacred is the spot !

[1] *See* Note F.

A spot so hallowed, so endeared,

    Is mine, a Chapel underground,

Where oft my spirit has been cheered,

    · My heart has solace found.

'T is like an ancient catacomb

    Where martyrs 'neath the altars sleep ;

Secluded, silent, as the Tomb

    Where Mary came to weep.

She seems to haunt the holy place,

    Brave, tender-hearted Magdalene,

A triumph of converting grace,

    Of penitents the queen.

'Rabboni, Master'—that is all

   Her lovely lips can find to say;

Her heart keeps love's own festival,

   An endless Easter Day.

And of the Twelve Apostles one

   Beside her stands, whose dazzled eyes

Would seem to gaze upon the sun

   In rapturous surprise.

Five rosy suns they see indeed,

   Arisen to dispel his night;

'My Lord, my God' is all the creed

   His trembling lips recite.

With Thomas and with Mary there

    Stand Saints and Angels side by side,

Encompassing the Sepulchre

    Of Jesus glorified ;

Encompassing His altar-throne

    Who in a Sacrament divine,

To make the Resurrection known,

    Turns water into wine.

Who seeks his spirit's lamp to feed,

    One with the Lord of Life must be ;

Discipleship is life indeed,

    Christ's slave alone is free.

Who loves and serves and follows Him

Need to no wilderness repair,

The Mercy-Seat and Cherubim

Confront him everywhere.

STUTTGART : 1889.

'*PARSIFAL.*'

(A Festival Play by Richard Wagner.)

> ' Glory and joy and honour to our Lord,
> And to the Holy Vessel of the Grail.'
> TENNYSON.

DEEP calleth unto deep—God's deep

To God-created depths in man ;

The hands that sow, the hands that reap,

Complete what His began.

For His the seed, and His the fruit,

And His the life at every stage ;

In God humanity strikes root,

Evolved from age to age.

From age to age the vision grows;

   Discerning eyes with wonder see

The desert blossom as the rose,

   God in humanity.

I hear a spirit-voice that calls

   To ears grown deaf, to hearts grown cold;

'T is music's spell, which still enthrals

   As sweetly as of old.

I find it wedded to the tale

   Oft told—a Gospel ever true—

The legend of the Holy Grail

   Interpreted anew.

Life conquers death in Parsifal,

 And Love, anointed priest and king,

Bids every heart keep festival,

 Bids all men pray and sing.

So evermore the vision grows ;

 Uplifted eyes with rapture see

The Chalice blushing as a rose

 Upon life's mystic Tree.[1]

Deep answers deep—an antiphon

 More clearly heard from age to age ;

For God and man in Christ are one,

 And God man's heritage.

BAYREUTH : *August* 15, 1888.

     [1] *See* Note G.

A CHRISTMAS FIRESIDE.

How dark these annual returns

  Of desolate Decembers!

The blackened Yule-log scarcely burns

  Upon the dying embers;

The frozen heart no longer yearns;

  Alas! it still remembers.

Does growing old mean growing cold?

  Must Love itself surrender?

If evening light lacks morning gold

And noon-day heat and splendour,

Does not the afterglow unfold

A secret sweet and tender ?

And lo ! the Christmas Star returns

That gladdened past Decembers ;

Again the Yule-log blazing burns

Above the glowing embers ;

A brighter hope my heart discerns

Than any it remembers.

S. Barnabas' : *Christmas Eve*, 1885.

PROLOGUE TO A CHRISTMAS PLAY.

PERFECTION is our final goal,
If love be undefeated :
Life then becomes a perfect whole,
And all things are completed.

Now trim the lamps and build the stage ;
To play needs preparation ;
Let art and taste and wit engage
To aid imagination.

Ah, there are brighter lights I know

(Though footlights, too, are pretty),

And to a broader stage we go,

The Spiritual City.

.   .   .   .   .

All, all things are related here,

The great things to the little ;

The toys our childhood held so dear

Are precious, if they 're brittle.

Our very playthings have their use,

A meaning hangs about them ;

Although I hold the man a goose

Who cannot live without them.

Blue is the dome, the carpet green,

When first the curtain's lifted ;

And bright and beautiful the scene,

The actors gay and gifted.

The dimpled queen of Babydom

Already is an actress ;

Each birth proclaims a kingdom come,

Earth owns her benefactress.

O'er every cradle shines a star

Of more than earthly brightness ;

And fairy-lamps the footlights are

That manifest its whiteness.

And so the play begins, and so
    Through five long acts advances,
With tears and laughter, weal and woe,
    Now dirges and now dances.

Life blends the bitter with the sweet,
    An undiscovered riddle;
And faster still the pulses beat
    When Cupid plays the fiddle.

.   .   .

Ah, there are sweeter sounds I know
    To golden harps vibrating ;
And to a fairer feast we go,
    The midnight cry awaiting.

Now comedy, now tragedy,

 The plot of life soon thickens ;

The heart, to-day so full of glee,

 To-morrow sinks and sickens.

So quickly shift the scenes, the dance

 Becomes a grave procession ;

But life is still the one romance,

 And love the one possession.

And, true to love, we find at last

 An end to the confusion,

A future brighter than the past,

 And happy the conclusion.

Ah, there are fairer lights I know

(Though footlights still are pretty,,

And there's a grander stage ; we go

To the Celestial City.

That lovely City stands four-square,

Its golden Gates are lifting ;

And when at length we enter there

The scene needs no more shifting.

Ah, when at last we reach that goal,

Delayed, but not defeated,

Our life shall be a rounded whole,

And love itself completed !

Christmas, 1888.

A CHRISTMAS CAROL

IN TWO PARTS AND A CONCLUSION.

PART I.

CONCERNING LOVE.

'When I passed by thee, and looked upon thee, behold, thy
time was the time of Love.'
'Love is of God.'

VERY sweet it is to play

With the name of Love, and say

'Love can never pass away.'

Love 's too faithful to forget ;

Have we learnt its secret yet—

'Love the gift is Love the debt'?

Love 's a Poet ; when he sings

Aspiration spreads her wings ;

Love transfigures common things.

Love 's an Angel sent to bless

Hearts forlorn and comfortless ;

Love 's the Champion of distress.

Love 's a Spirit pure and free,

Bowing head and bending knee

At the shrine of Chastity.

Love 's a Potentate who reigns

Crowned and sceptred ; Love disdains

Crooked ways and sordid gains.

Love's a Red Cross Knight ; unseen,

Life and Death he rides between,

Guardian of a pilgrim-queen.

Love's a Prophet in disguise ;

Souls courageous, faithful, wise,

Love is quick to canonise.

Love's a Lamb, a Turtle-dove ;

Love is throned all thrones above,

For the Name of God is ' Love.'

PART II.

CONCERNING JESUS.

'The WORD was made Flesh, and dwelt among us, and we
beheld His Glory.'
' Unto us a Child is born.'
' His Name was called JESUS.'

LOVE 'S a Babe, from Heaven bringing

Gifts, what time the bells are ringing,

Prelude to the carol-singing.

Love, down-stooping, lays His Head,

With His Baby-arms outspread,

Infant-wise in Manger-bed.

Love 's the Ruler of the Feast ;

Since His Star rose in the East

How the Sunshine has increased !

Love 's the Healer, His the skill

All our sicknesses to kill,

His the power, His the will.

Love 's a Warrior renowned,

When the battle rages round,

And the Gospel Trumpets sound.

Love with unaffrighted eyes

Looks on Death, unmasks, defies,

Ah ! 't is Death, not Love, that dies !

Love 's a Priest, whose wounded feet

Stand where Earth and Heaven meet,

Lifting up a Censer sweet.

Love, so blessing and so blest,

Finding there His food and rest,

Nestles to a Maiden's breast.

Sweet it is to sing and say

' Love can never pass away,

Born for us on Christmas Day.'

CONCLUSION.

CONCERNING LIFE.

(TO ANY CHILD.)

' In Him was Life, and the Life was the Light of men.'

'Jesus rejoiced in spirit and said, I thank **Thee**, O Father, Lord of heaven and earth, that Thou hast hid these things from the wise and prudent, and hast revealed them unto babes.'

BELIEVE me, life is very sweet,

If in His Steps we plant our feet

Whose Cradle is the Mercy-Seat.

So, homeward-bound, we all may stand

One happy day at Love's Right Hand,

And see at last our Fatherland.

The child is evermore the seer

To whom the hidden things appear,

Obedience makes the vision clear.

But very hard it is to tell

What visions mean ; no eyes see well

That see not things invisible.

'T is not a mask we see, a blind,

But veil transparent ; and behind

A lovely Countenance we find.

The love-light in the Father's Eye

On all things falls ; His babes thereby

May know what visions signify.

But, to *discern* the things you see,

Both child and prophet you must be,

Fulfilled of peace and purity.[1]

Your head an aureole must wear,

God's Smile such sunshine makes, and where

It falls there beats the pulse of prayer.

Your heart must be a living thing,

Alert, upsoaring, carolling,

Like happy bird upon the wing.

Your hands, empowered from above,

Like Noah's sending forth the dove,

Must be the ministers of Love.

[1] *See* Note II.

Your feet the homeward path must tread,

And, bleeding, bruise the serpent's head,

By angel-guards companionèd.

Ah, what a vision, heaven-sent,

Accompanied the Dove's descent

When JESUS to the Jordan went !

Of that you too may be the seer,

To childhood heaven lies so near,

And Love makes every vision clear.

Yes, life is wonderfully sweet,

If we but clasp and kiss the Feet

Of One in whom all graces meet :

I

Of One, the Fairest of the fair,

Who His Inheritance would share

With all His brothers everywhere.

If we but answer to His call,

And at His Feet adoring fall,

Life's fever is Love's festival.

The vision brightens with the years,

More fair it shines beheld through tears,

Most fair when all else disappears.

The vision lasts, the rapture grows :

The veil, when lifted, shall disclose

Things that we know not ; JESUS knows

And so our hearts shall dance and sing,

And loud shall be the carolling

Around the Cradle of our King.

S. Barnabas' : *Christmas*, 1887.

THE END

THE end ? Ah, no! it is an endless end

Towards which all things that live for ever tend,

Returning ever to their secret source,

The spring inviolate of vital force.

And whosoever lives must needs dispense

Life's water, else condemned to impotence ;

Unauthorised is he to speak or sing

Whose uttered word is not a living thing.

Love is, I trust, the author of my book,

And I, Love's vassal, do not blush to look

My reader in the face, and say to him—

Weak though my voice may be, my vision dim,

My meaning holds a music which, if heard,

Will make amends for every halting word.

Hark to a heart-pulse, throbbing to the beat

Of measured words,—a whisper faint and sweet,

Yet loud enough perchance for Love to hear—

Love of the questing heart and questioning ear ;

And competent one secret to proclaim,

Hope's gospel, in one world-redeeming Name.

BETCHWORTH : 1889.

NOTES

NOTE A, p. 33.

Of Columbus, Prescott says :—' He seemed too much absorbed by the great cause to which he had consecrated his life, to allow scope for the lower pursuits and pleasures which engage ordinary men.' Lord Tennyson, in the pathetic poem that bears his name, has given vivid expression to the enthusiasm that fired the heart of the great adventurer and shaped his heroic career, his life-long and passionate devotion, in spite of all disappointments, indignities, and reverses, to the Catholic cause. He was a true Crusader. No life has more forcibly illustrated the truth of Montaigne's words— ' Malheur à celui qui est en avance de son siècle ! '

NOTE B, p. 36.

The following is Prescott's account of the incident to which my verses refer—one of the most romantic pages surely of a romantic history : —

' As the column under the Grand Cardinal advanced up the Hill of Martyrs, over which a road had been constructed for the passage of the artillery, he was met by the Moorish Prince Abdallah, attended by fifty cavaliers, who, descending the hill, rode up to the position occupied by Ferdinand on the banks of the Xen l. As the Moor approached the Spanish King, he would have thrown himself from his horse, and saluted his hand in token of homage, but Ferdinand hastily prevented him, embracing him with every mark of sympathy and regard. Abdallah then delivered up the keys of the Alhambra to his conqueror, saying, "They are thine, O King, since Allah so decrees it ; use thy success with clemency and moderation."

' Ferdinand would have uttered some words of consolation to the unfortunate Prince, but he moved forward with a dejected air to the spot occupied by Isabella, and, after similar acts of obeisance, passed on to join his family, who had preceded him with his most valuable effects on the route to Alpujarras. The Sovereigns during this time waited with impatience the signal of the occupation of the city by the Cardinal's troop, which, winding slowly along the outer circuit of the walls as previously arranged, in order to spare the feelings of the citizens as far as possible, entered by what is now called the Gate of Los Molinos. In a short time the large silver cross, borne by Ferdinand throughout the crusade, was seen sparkling in the sunbeams, while the standards of Castile and St. Iago waved triumphantly from the red towers of the Alhambra. At this glorious spectacle, the choir of the royal chapel broke forth into the solemn anthem of the *Te Deum* ; and the whole army, penetrated with deep emotion, prostrated themselves on their knees in adoration of the Lord of Hosts, who had at length granted the consummation of their wishes in this last and glorious triumph of the Cross. The grandees who surrounded Ferdinand then advanced towards the Queen, and kneeling down, saluted her hand in token of homage to her as Sovereign of Granada. The procession took up its march towards the city, "the King and Queen moving in the midst," says an historian, "emblazoned with royal magnificence; and as they were now in the prime of life, and had now achieved the completion of this glorious conquest, they seemed to represent even more than their wonted majesty. Equal with each other, they were raised far above the rest of the world. They appeared, indeed, more than mortal, and as if sent by heaven for the salvation of Spain."

'In the meanwhile the Moorish King, traversing the route of the Alpujarras, reached a rocky eminence which commanded a last view of Granada. He checked his horse, and, as his eyes for the last time wandered over the scenes of his departed greatness, his heart swelled, and he burst into tears.

'"You do well," said his more masculine mother, "to weep like a woman, for what you could not defend like a man."

'"Alas!" exclaimed the unhappy exile, "when were woes ever equal to mine!"

'The scene of this event is still pointed out to the traveller by the people of the district; and the rocky height from which the Moorish chief took his sad farewell of the princely abodes of his youth is commemorated by the poetical title of

'"El último Sospiro del Moro,"

'"The last Sigh of the Moor."'

(*Ferdinand and Isabella*, vol. i. pp. 451-453. London, 1867.)

Note C, p. 57.

The idea of *duality* is nowhere more beautifully expressed than in a remarkable passage, too long for quotation, of Mr. Pater's *Marius the Epicurean*, vol. ii. pp. 71-77. My readers will, I think, be grateful for the reference.

Note D, p. 82.

Some beautiful verses—*A Walk in a Churchyard*—by Archbishop Trench, give fuller and worthier expression to this thought. I made their acquaintance after my poem was written.

Note E, p. 85.

I cannot deny myself the pleasure of extracting the following beautiful passage from Canon Westcott's little book, *Gifts for Ministry* :—' How those two words of S. Paul, " *in Christ*," give a solid foundation to the vague feeling after the fatherhood of God and the brotherhood of men, which is at present the pathetic expression of " souls naturally Christian." How they come back to us when we are baffled, wearied, discouraged, with minds darkened

by clouds of human misery and crime, and eyes dimmed by strain-
ing for the dawn. *In Christ* : here lies the fresh spring of wisdom
and understanding. *In Christ* nothing is lost, nothing is in-
effective, nothing dies but that it may rise to a more fertile life.
In Christ our least glimpse of the Truth falls into its due place in
the limitless prospect of the love of God. *In Christ* our least
labour becomes a part of a Divine ministry.' (Page 24.)

Note F, p. 88.

The Chapel of the Holy Sepulchre to which my verses refer is
in the crypt of S. Barnabas' Church, immediately underneath the
sanctuary—the most secluded spot, I think, in all London. For this
beautiful addition to a beautiful church I am indebted to the genius
of Mr. Bodley. It enshrines the original altar of S. Barnabas',
famous in the annals of the Catholic Revival, which, after many
years of disuse, has been now again reinstated, not indeed in its old
position, but (as it were) in an inner chamber, and with all befitting
dignity and adornment. It was first used again on the Sunday in
the Octave of Dedication, 1887, when the Bishop of Lincoln
celebrated the Holy Eucharist there, and has ever since been in
constant use.

There are in the little chapel three small and deeply recessed
windows ; the one over the altar represents Christ on the Cross ;
the other two S. Mary Magdalene and S. Thomas respectively,

as being specially the Saints of Easter Day and Low Sunday. The legend under the Magdalene is as follows :—*Eripuit animam meam de morte, oculos meos a lacrymis* ; that under Didymus, *Ut credentes vitam habeatis in Nomine ejus.* The reredos represents the Annunciation on two painted panels, and opposite the altar is a canopied seat with a panel-picture of the Entombment. The walls and vaulted roof are enriched with various scriptures, scrolls, and legends, those of most frequent recurrence being the old Catholic prayers, *Jesu Mercy* and *Requiem æternam dona eis, Domine.* A floor of black and white marble dimly reflects the light of the sanctuary lamp.

Mr. Shields is at work upon a picture, representing the women-worshippers in the Garden of the Sepulchre, which will shortly be placed on the wall of the ante-chapel. The frontispiece of this book is a photograph of it.

Note G, p. 95.

The following suggestive lines are from the pen of Mr. Morris :—

' A fair and mystic Tree
Rose like a heart in shape, and 'mid its leaves
One golden mystic fruit with a fair seed
Hid in it. This, with childish hand, I took
And ate, and straight I knew the tree was Life,
And the fruit Death, and the hid seed was Love.'
The Epic of Hades : Persephone.

NOTE II, p. 112.

The child is always and everywhere a seer ; and not unfre-
quently he is empowered all unconsciously to declare and interpret
the vision that his eyes behold—a poet and prophet as well. No one
has realised this more vividly perhaps than Novalis ; ' The first
man,' he says, ' is the first spirit-seer ; all appears to him as spirit.
What are children but first men ? The fresh gaze of the child is
richer in significance than the forecasting of the most indubitable
seer.' It is interesting—painfully interesting—to remember that
the Sophie, so passionately loved by him, and whose death left him
so soon desolate, was only thirteen when he first saw her, and died
two days after her fifteenth birthday.

What childhood in its prophetic mood thinks and sees and feels,
let Emerson tell us in the following lines of his *Mayday*:—

> ' And ever, when the happy child,
> In May beholds the blooming wild,
> And hears in heaven the blue-bird sing,
> " Onward," he cries, " your baskets bring !
> In the next field is air more mild,
> And in yon hazy west is Eden's balmier spring." '

PRINTED BY
SPOTTISWOODE AND CO., NEW-STREET SQUARE
LONDON